Molly Make Yourself Big

Shari Harpaz

First Edition Book, 2023

ISBN 978-1-957506-58-6 - paperback
ISBN 978-1-957506-61-6 - Case laminate
ISBN 978-1-957506-59-3 - ebook

Published by Skinny Brown Dog Media Atlanta, GA
www.skinnybrowndogmedia.com
Distributed by Skinny Brown Dog Media

Dedication

Casey: You're my heart, my soul, my inspiration and my dream come true. I'm so lucky to be your mommy. I love you so big!
Be Brave, Be Kind, Stand Tall and Always Be You.

Mom & Dad: Your unconditional love and support have given me the courage to follow my dreams and the strength to get back up when I fall.
Thank you for always being my biggest cheerleaders!

Molly couldn't fall asleep. Tomorrow would be her first day at a new school. Every time she closed her eyes, Molly imagined a giant monster chasing her around the classroom. As the monster stomped closer, she felt as if she was becoming smaller and smaller.

"Mommy, what if nobody wants to be my friend? What if someone is mean to me?" Molly worried.

"I know starting a new school feels scary. Your teacher will be there to help you. Just be yourself and I'm sure you'll make friends quickly." Mom stroked her hair and began to sing their special song.

"My sweet little girl. I wish for you the world. Be brave and strong and kind. And always speak your mind. I'll catch you when you fall.

"...ust always stand up tall. No matter what you do, Know that I will always love you..."

Molly's eyes slowly closed and she drifted off to sleep.

The next morning, when Molly was getting ready, her body felt like butterflies were dancing all over her skin.

Everything she put on felt itchy and pokey. "Mommy, Mommy, where is my favorite dress? I can't find it anywhere," she cried.

"It's right here," her mom said as she entered the room holding Molly's tie-dyed dress.

Molly's mom knelt beside her, held her hands and they began to take long, slow breaths. Soon her body relaxed and Molly quickly got dressed for school.

"Sweetheart, I have a little surprise for you for your first day. It will remind you to be brave and kind and everything will work out fine. Close your eyes and no peeking." Molly eagerly closed her eyes as her mom gently placed something around her neck.

When she opened her eyes, Molly squealed as she saw the beautiful necklace that said BRAVE on one side and KIND on the other. She felt ready to go to school!

Outside the school, teachers greeted the children with warm, welcoming smiles. Molly's teacher took her hand and led a group of students inside to their classroom.

After hanging up her backpack, Molly found the table with her name tag. She was seated between a friendly girl named Julia and a funny boy named Drew.

In the morning, the class did fun get-to-know-you activities. They colored "All About Me" pictures and took turns sharing their favorite hobbies. Drew loved talking about all sorts of creepy crawlers!

When it was Molly's turn, she showed everyone the "Let Me Tell You What I Like" dance, which she used to do at her old school. The class had so much fun and wanted to do it over and over again!

At lunchtime, they even had food that was shaped like animals. Molly loved the bear-shaped grilled cheese and the frog-shaped cucumbers. This new school was awesome!

During recess, Molly was happily running around playing tag with Julia, Drew and some other kids from her class.

She was thinking about what a great day she was having when a ball suddenly hit her hard on the back. It really hurt. "Ouch," Molly groaned.

Molly turned to see who kicked the ball and there, just a few feet away, stood a boy glaring at her with scary eyes and a smirk.

Feeling frightened, Molly wished she could hide. She quickly lowered her gaze, hunched her shoulders and scurried away from the scary-looking boy.

For the rest of the day, Molly nervously kept looking over her shoulder. She couldn't wait for the school bell to ring.

Finally it was time to go home. Molly slowly walked outside and saw her mom waiting for her. "How was your first day?", her mom asked eagerly. Molly quietly whispered, "It was fine." Her mom could tell that something was wrong.

In the car, Molly's mom tried again, "What was your favorite part of your day? Did you make any new friends?" Usually, Molly was very chatty after a day at school, but today she sat in the back of the car silently staring out the window.

When Molly got home, her little dog Rosy jumped into her arms and showered her face with wet doggie kisses. "Oh Wigglebutt, you're the best little girl," Molly giggled while wiping her cheeks. "Waawooo," Rosy howled between licks.

Snuggling Rosy, Molly walked into the kitchen where her mom was preparing an after-school snack.

"Mommy, today school started off great, but at recess it turned scary. There was a boy on the playground who acted like a monster. First, he threw a ball at me, and then he kept pushing me whenever he had a chance."

Her mom knelt down. "Molly, do you remember what we practiced? When someone treats you unkindly, you need to MAKE YOURSELF BIG. Stand tall, use a strong voice, look them in the eyes, and say, "DON'T DO THAT AGAIN." Her mom gave her a reassuring hug and gently kissed her head.

The rest of the evening, Molly practiced making herself big. With each try, she felt more confident. When Molly stood up tall, she was able to find her strong, courageous voice. She said "DON'T DO THAT AGAIN" one last time before she ran and hugged her mom good night. "I love you, my brave, kind girl. Sweet dreams."

The next morning, as Molly walked into school, she felt a mix of emotions. She was a little nervous about facing "that boy," but excited to see Julia and Drew. Taking a deep breath, she slowly stepped into her classroom.

Julia and Drew were already at the table working on their morning activities. "Hi Molly. Come color with us," they called out when they saw her.

As Molly walked towards her friends, a foot suddenly appeared and tripped her. She stumbled and fell, feeling surprised and embarrassed. That same boy, who had frightened her on her first day, was looking down at her and snickering.

Molly felt tears stinging her eyes but then, her mom's voice echoed in her mind, "MAKE YOURSELF BIG!"

She took a deep breath, wiped her tears away, and stood up tall. She put her shoulders back, hands on her hips, looked the boy straight in the eyes and said, "DON'T DO THAT AGAIN."

Molly felt empowered as she stood tall and locked eyes with the boy.

As she stood her ground, something surprising happened. The boy didn't look like a monster anymore. He looked like a worried, little boy unsure of what to do next.

"I'm s...orry," said the boy, his lip quivering. "I w..on't do it again. Um, Hi, my name is Ben."

Molly wasn't sure how to respond. She didn't know if she could trust Ben, but she also believed that everybody deserves a second chance. Touching her necklace, she was reminded that she could be both brave and kind at the same time. She cautiously replied, "My name is Molly."

At the end of the school day, Molly happily skipped towards her mom, as her new friends shouted and waved, "See you tomorrow, Molly!"

Molly's Special Song

Shari Harp

♩ = 103

My swe et lit tle (girl/boy). I wish for you the world. Be brave be strong be kind.

And al ways speak your mind. I'll catch you when you fall. Just al ways stand up tall.

No ma tter what you do. Know that I will al ways love you.

CPSIA information can be obtained
at www.ICGtesting.com
Printed in the USA
JSHW061102210523
41981JS00002B/4

9 781957 506616